TOO MANY MONSTERS

BY EVE BUNTING

ILLUSTRATED BY JAMES BERNARDIN

Troll

BridgeWater Books

TO MY LUNCH BUNCH MONSTERS. —E. B.

FOR LiTTLE WYETH JAMES,
MAY YOU HAVE A QUACK FOR
EVERY MONSTER. —J. B.

Text copyright © 2001 by Eve Bunting.
Illustrations copyright © 2001 by James Bernardin.

Published by BridgeWater Books, an imprint and registered trademark of Troll Communications L.L.C.

Printed in Hong Kong.

10 9 8 7 6 5 4 3 2 1

Library of Congress Cataloging-in-Publication Data

Bunting, Eve, 1928 -
    Too many monsters / by Eve Bunting ; illustrated by James Bernardin.
       p.   cm.
    Summary: A young boy is frightened by the monsters that show up in his room at bedtime,
until his parents show him how to get rid of them.
    ISBN 0-8167-7178-2
    [1. Bedtime-Fiction. 2. Monsters-Fiction. 3. Fear-Fiction.] I. Bernardin, James, ill. II. Title.

PZ7.B91527 Tp 2001
[E]-dc21   00-066342

After Mom had tucked me in bed and turned out the lights, I realized there were a lot of monsters in my room.

There was one sitting on my dresser, reading my train book and swinging his legs.

There was one in my chair,
painting his toenails.

There was a long, thin one under my bed,
eating popcorn.

There was a round one
bouncing my tennis ball
against my wall.

There was one bumping around in my closet, doing who knows what.

I went downstairs.

Mom and Dad sat at the kitchen table, eating pie.

I sat next to them in my own place.

"There are too many monsters in my room," I said.

Dad looked worried. "That's not good."

Mom gave me a small piece of pie on my blue plate.

We sat, munching and thinking.

"Did you know monsters are very afraid of ducks?" Mom asked.

Dad nodded. "It's the quacking that scares them."

"I didn't know that," I said.

Then I had an idea. "Let's go upstairs and pretend to be ducks."

"Unfortunately," Dad said, "we don't look much like ducks."

"But it's the quacking that scares them," I explained.

"I think I knew that," Dad said.

We went upstairs.

"Are they still in there?" Mom asked. "I don't quite see them."

"Oh, yes," I told her. "They're all over the place. Grown-ups can't see monsters. Just kids can see them."

"I didn't know that," Mom said.

Dad opened my window wide. "Are we ready?" he asked.
"One, two, three."

"Wow," I said when we stopped for breath.
"These monsters are leaving in a hurry!"

First, the one who'd been sitting on my dresser, reading my train book and swinging his legs, rushed for the window.

The one who'd been in my
chair, painting his toenails,
rushed after him.

Then the long, thin one who'd been
under my bed, eating popcorn, left.

Then the round one who'd been
bouncing my tennis ball against the wall.

Then the one who'd been bumping around in my closet,
doing who knows what.

"Whew!" I said.

"They've all gone."

"Thank goodness," Mom said.

I snuggled down in my
bed and waited to be
tucked in again.

"Those monsters definitely won't
be back," Dad told me.

"I know that," I said. "Too many ducks!"